By

Kristin Cole Brown

Illustrated by

Matt Maley

Dance on!

Kristin Brown

all my love — Miss Lisa

ISBN-13: 978-1981186754
ISBN-10: 1981186751

My mama is always working, but not always in the same place.

Once she worked at a grocery store

Then at a fancy hotel.

Sometimes she works at the hospital.

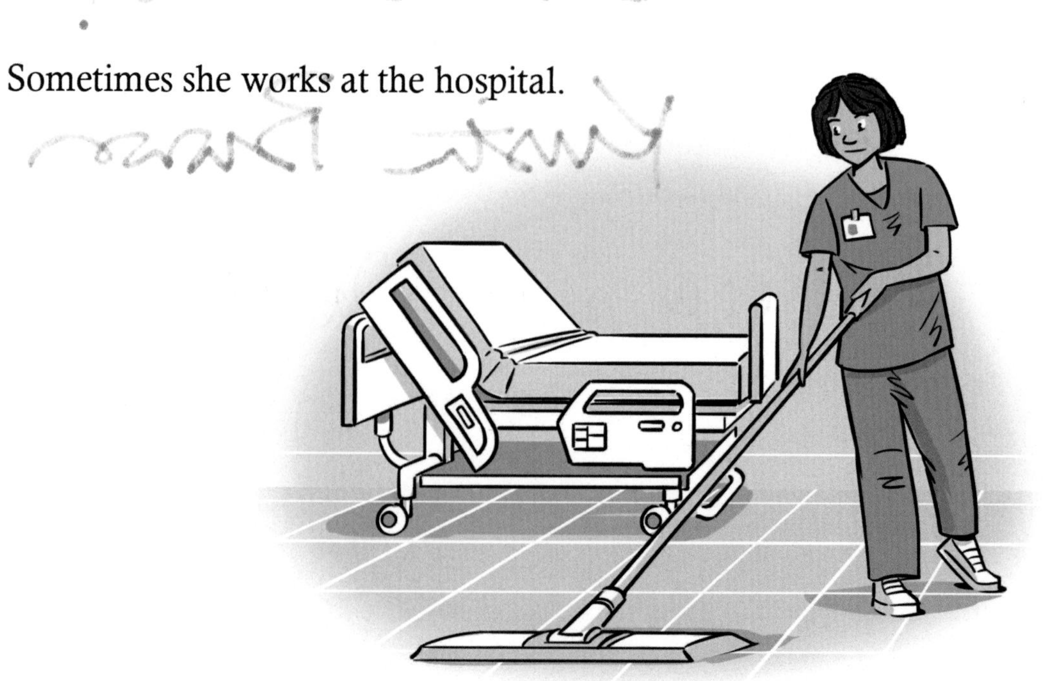

But when Mama isn't working, she does her happy dance.

Mama's best job is for a lady named Marguerite.

This is ***my*** favorite job.

Because Mama always has time after work to take me to soccer practice!

I have practice every day.

Not to brag, but I'm the top scorer on our team.

Last week Marguerite invited us over for Thanksgiving Dinner.

There were so many leftovers Mama didn't have to cook for three days!

After dinner, Marguerite put on some music from a ballet called ***The Nutcracker.*** Marguerite dances the part of the Grandmother in the ballet!

She showed us how to dance the polka. Mama picked it up quicker than anybody.

Marguerite sits on the board of *The Nutcracker*.

(Mama explained it's not an actual board.)

I've never been to the ballet before,
so I was so excited when Marguerite
helped Mama get a job as an usher...

at ***The Nutcracker!***

I've seen it **ten times** so far!

I really wanted to help backstage, but Rex said no.
Rex is the theater manager.
Kids aren't allowed to work.
Instead, he gave me a tour
and told me all about how a theater works.

I know everything seems like magic on TV, but when you see it in real life, it's like you're ***inside*** the magic. The ballerinas prance on their toes and the boys lift them as easy as anything.

One of the boys
leaps around the stage
about fifteen times!
Everyone claps like crazy.

The children in the Nutcracker story get dancing dolls for Christmas presents.

My favorites are the Russian Dolls.

The music makes me want to dance with them!

And the Chinese Dolls look like they're having so much fun!

But *everyone* loves the Sugar Plum Fairy.
A lady named Eliza dances the part.
You should see all the flowers she gets
at curtain call!

Eliza is so nice! One man always gives her gynormous bouquets of stargazers.
After the show she gives some to me and Mama, and donates the rest to the hospital.

The flowers make our whole bus smell like candy!

Sometimes we hand them out to people who look sad or lonely.

We dance the polka all the way down the last block.

If we're too tired to dance, we'll talk about our day.

Once Marguerite told Mama *"You walk like a ballerina."*
That's when I found out Mama took ballet classes when she was my age.

Marguerite asked if I ever wanted to take ballet lessons,
but there's no way I'd give up playing soccer.
However, now I know what I want to be for Halloween next year.

SUGAR PLUM ZOMBIE TUTU DEFENDER!

Marguerite took us to lunch one day and called me a ***smart cookie***.

"Because you will always be able to play soccer with your friends. ***-sigh-*** *Thank goodness I can still dance the Grandmother. I'd rather play a small part in The Nutcracker than no part at all! And it's such a happy part!"*

Turns out Marguerite used to play the Sugar Plum Fairy!

"I could still get up on my toes in those days."

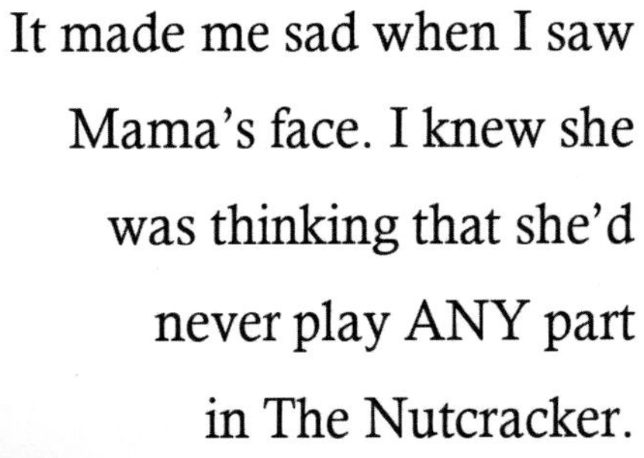

It made me sad when I saw Mama's face. I knew she was thinking that she'd never play ANY part in The Nutcracker.

Last Sunday when we got to the theater, Rex was very worried.

Nobody had seen Marguerite!

Just then, his phone rang.

"Marguerite, where are you?

...What?? Are you serious?

Your understudy has the flu!

I'll never find a sub now!...

Really, she does?

Well, why not?"

Suddenly Rex grabbed our hands. *"Come with me!"*

He took us back stage and called for Desmond, the costume designer.

"She sprained her ankle on her way here."

Desmond looked like he would faint. *"Who's the sub?"*

Rex said, *"Right here."* Desmond looked around. *"Where?"*

Suddenly Mama smiled.

Rex took my hand and said, *"Let's find you a special seat."*

I always wondered who gets to sit in those boxes above the audience. That's me and Marguerite!

The lights dimmed, and Rex stepped into the spotlight center stage.

I clapped so loud when he said my Mama's name, I thought my hands would fall off.

During the Christmas Party scene when all the guests were arriving, there was Mama, doing the polka with her partner.

Her partner looked a little surprised when he lifted her off the ground.

Marguerite's ankle still hurt, so Mama ended up dancing the Grandmother in every performance after that. One day Marguerite brought in a newspaper. The headline read *"Dancing Like a Star."* And there was a picture of Mama in the middle of a twirl. Underneath it said: *"Grandmother captures our hearts."* The article was all about Mama's jobs and how she got to dance, and how Rex let me sit in the special box.

After that, the clapping was extra loud
when Mama entered the stage.
I was so proud I felt like a doll
full of stuffing that just had to burst out.

Today was the final performance. Fancy cars were driving up and people stepped out looking like they were going to the Academy Awards. I never saw such beautiful clothes on actual people before.

It was the day before Christmas,

and the theater was decorated with millions of lights.

Marguerite gave me and Mama the best Christmas present ever:
Corner Kick seats to the Women's Nationals next year!

Eliza walked by and whispered, "I've got a surprise for you." I ***begged*** her to tell me, but she just smiled and ducked backstage.

The curtain rose to show the children getting ready for the party. The guests arrived, and Mama held a fan this time.

Sheesh. Was ***that*** the surprise?

Nope.

I love curtain calls! You get to clap extra hard for your favorite dancers. When it was Eliza's turn, people yelled ***"Brava! Bravissima!"*** and threw so many flowers the stage looked like a garden of Stargazers.

Then Eliza placed her finger to her lips. The theater became quiet. It was time for the final curtain call, when everyone takes a bow together. But tonight, the curtains parted and Eliza walked through the opening and came back out - holding Mama's hand!

Suddenly Rex walked on stage
and presented Mama with her own bouquet of Stargazers.
Then Mama made the deepest, most perfect curtsy I ever saw.

She told me later to look up the words “flustered,
overwhelmed and surreal” to understand how she felt.

When we got home, Mama kicked her off her shoes and pulled me down next to her on the couch.

“Honey, I think you and I are in a real life fairy tale.”

She gave me a squeeze.

“But the sweetest part of all is having a Sugar Plum Zombie Tutu Defender by my side every day.”

So that's my story!

I hope you love the Nutcracker as much as Mama and I do.

See you there!

The end.

For my Mama.

Many thanks to my family for their patient, nail-on-the-head, editorial review; to Peter and Lisa Naumann of the *New Paltz Ballet Theatre* for helping me avoid what would have been catastrophic bloopers; and to Matt Maley for so perfectly capturing the heart of this story.

Kristin Cole Brown is married to David Smith,
has two grown children and five grandchildren.
She grew up in New York City where she studied ballet under André,
Afro Modern Dance with Syvilla Fort and the Fox Trot with Miss Parnova.

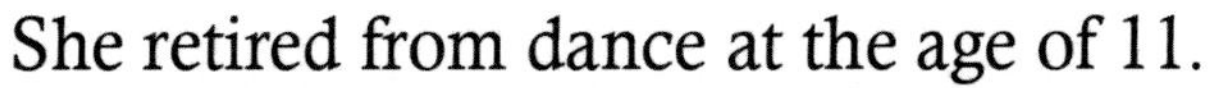

She retired from dance at the age of 11.

Matt Maley is an Illustrator, Graphic Artist and Sculptor
living in New Paltz, NY. with his family and pets.
He briefly played "The King"
in a 4th grade performance of *The King And I.*
His mom used an old curtain to make the pants.
The King was not pleased.

mattmaley.com

Made in the USA
Middletown, DE
07 December 2017